W9-BUD-143

ONE
MEAN
ANT
WITH
FLY
AND
FLEA
AND
MOTH

For Jim, Sigourney, and Char,
my dearest friends

AY

To Pip and Selma

SR

Text copyright © 2021 by Arthur Yorinks
Illustrations copyright © 2021 by Sergio Ruzzier

All rights reserved. No part of this book may be reproduced, transmitted, or stored in an information
retrieval system in any form or by any means, graphic, electronic, or mechanical, including photocopying,
taping, and recording, without prior written permission from the publisher.

First edition 2021

Library of Congress Catalog Card Number pending
ISBN 978-0-7636-8396-2

21 22 23 24 25 26 CCP 10 9 8 7 6 5 4 3 2 1

Printed in Shenzhen, Guangdong, China

This book was typeset in ITC American Typewriter.
The illustrations were done in pen and ink and watercolor.

Candlewick Press
99 Dover Street
Somerville, Massachusetts 02144

www.candlewick.com

ONE MEAN ANT

WITH

FLY AND FLEA

AND MOTH

written by
Arthur Yorinks

illustrated by
Sergio Ruzzier

CANDLEWICK PRESS

R0461185980

"LADIES AND GENTLEMEN AND KIDS OF ALL AGES!"
announced Big Jim, the ringleader of Jim's Flea
Circus. "Right here, right now—I give you—
Ant and Fly and Flea!"

Yes, there they were—an ant, a fly, and a flea—the top bananas, the headliners, the stars of the circus!

Sounds kind of glamorous, right?

Wrong.

Still, showbiz is not kind. After their exhausting performance, the ant, the fly, and the flea would return to their meager cage, with only a drop of sugar water and a crumb, *one crumb*, for meals. No day off. No rest. No nothing.

No, it was a miserable life for one mean ant and his friends, a fly and a flea. Every night, and twice on Sundays, they had to perform death-defying circus acts.

In the center of a ring of fire, the ant would lift the fly above his head with the flea balanced on top of the fly's nose. Wow. But wait!

Then, in a boffo finish, the fly would throw the ant up in the air while the flea jumped from the fly's face, did a triple somersault, and landed perfectly on the ant's back. Spectacular!

"I'm starving," moaned the flea. "We've got to get out of here!"

"Save your breath," grumbled the mean ant. "There's no way out, we're prisoners, we're doomed, and it's all your fault."

"My fault?" asked the flea. "You're the one who led us in the wrong direction. I said, 'Don't go that way, we'll end up in the flea circus.' And you said, 'No, we won't,' and I said, 'We will, too,' and you said, 'No, we won't,' and I said, 'Yes, we will,' and you said—"

"Enough!" bellowed the ant.

You see, the ant, the fly, and the flea were once all stuck in a spider's web, about to be eaten by a spider, when, well—that's another story.

"Just when I thought I was out of the flea circus," muttered the flea, "I was pulled back in. By, by . . . by *you*! You, you, you!"

"Who? Me?" yelled the ant.

"Yes, you!" shouted the flea.

"Well, if it weren't for me, we'd be in the middle of nowhere," said the ant. "I dragged us—"

"Right into Big Jim's hand!" said the flea. "Look at us, all stuck in this cage with no food. Look at me! I look like, like . . ."

"A flea?" asked the ant.

"Exactly, a fl . . . Well, of course I look like a flea!" said the flea. "I *am* a flea. And you're a, you're a—" A lot of awful words were in the flea's head.

"Don't say it, don't even think it," said the ant.

"You're a—"

Whew, the flea almost said . . . no, I can't say it either.

"Listen, fellas," interrupted the fly, trying to make peace. "It's not so bad. All right, okay, we live in a cage, we're forced to work seven days a week, but at least we have a better act than the moth."

"The moth?" cried the ant. "You call that an act? What kind of act is that? They turn on a light bulb and he flies right into it."

"Don't you know anything?" asked the flea. "It's a comedy act."

"I don't think it's funny," said the ant.

"I think it's hilarious," said the fly. "When he hits his head on the bulb. Boing!" The fly began to laugh. "It's, it's hysterical." The flea started to laugh, too.

"He, he does it every time! BOING!" The flea and the fly were howling with laughter.

"QUIET!" screamed the ant. "You're both nuts. Here we are, in this flea-infested— uh, no offense."

"None taken," said the flea.

"Here we are, trapped like rats—"

"Are they in the circus, too?" asked the fly.

"No, no, it's an expression!" moaned the ant. "Oh, how did I ever get mixed up with you two?"

"Well, first you were lost in the desert and I said I could fly us out and then—" began the fly.

"No, no! It wasn't a real question," said the ant.

"Sounded like a real question to me," said the flea.

"I think it was a real question," said the fly.

"Oh, I can't take this," said the ant. "I have to get out of here."

"That's what *I* said," said the flea. "And then you said—"

"STOP!" The ant was so aggravated he started banging his head on the floor, which naturally woke up their roommate. The moth.

"Uh, hi," said the moth. "What are you all talking about?"

"We were discussing," explained the fly, "how we have to get out of here."

"Oh," said the moth. "Why?"

"Why?" asked the mean ant. "Because we're trapped like—because we're—oh, I give up."

"Well, giving up won't get you anywhere," said the moth. "I had an aunt who used to say—"

"Who cares!" the ant, the flea, *and* the fly all said at once.

"That's not what she said," said the moth. "She never said 'who cares,' not ever."

"Look, Moth," said the ant, trying to control his temper. "We don't care what your aunt said. All we care about is getting out of here. You know, there's more to life than light bulbs!"

"There is?" asked the moth. "I don't think so. I see the light, I like the light."

"The moth likes the light," echoed the flea. "Everybody knows that."

"That's it!" cried the ant.

"What's it?" asked the fly.

"I don't know," said the moth.

"I've got it!" exclaimed the ant.

"What's he got, what's he got?" asked the moth.

"Cuckoo-itis," said the flea. "From banging his head so much."

"No," said the ant. "I've got a plan, I've got a plan to get us out of here!"

"Really?" asked the fly. "Where is it?"

"Where's what?" asked the ant.

"The plan!" said the fly.

"In my head!" said the ant.

"Oh, great," said the flea. "Forget it."

"He forgot his own plan?" asked the moth.

The ant started banging his head on the floor again.

"Is that the plan?" asked the fly.

"I told you the plan stunk," said the flea. "We're still here. It's not working."

"It's NOT THE PLAN!" the ant yelled. "Look, here's the plan. At tomorrow's performance, when the moth sees the light, instead of flying to it, he flies *away* from it."

"I don't get it," said the flea.

"Everyone expects the moth to fly toward the light," explained the ant. "But he doesn't."

"So," said the flea.

"So, Big Jim will look at the light to see what's going on, and when he does, the moth will grab the flea, while the fly will grab me, and we'll all fly away!"

"The fly flies with the flea?" asked the moth.

"No, no, no, the fly flies with me while you fly with the flea," said the ant.

"You mean, the flea takes you, and—" the fly began.

"NO!" yelled the ant. "The flea goes with me, I mean, the fly flies with—oh, forget it! Here, let's practice."

The ant gave the signal, and the fly switched on the light. The moth flew right into it.

"He doesn't get it," said the flea.

"We're doomed," said the fly.

"I can do it, I can!" said the moth. "Give me another chance."

"The flashlight is out. I think the battery is dead," said the fly.

"So are we," mumbled the flea.

"I can do it!" said the moth.

The ant, the fly, and the flea all thought the worst. Especially the flea.

The next day arrived and like every other day, the circus music rang out. The ant, the fly, and the flea were offstage, while the moth was ready for his entrance.

The drumroll began. The light bulb lit up. The moth rose into the air. Higher and higher he went, and . . . and . . . he flew *away* from the light!

There was a hush! The music stopped!
Big Jim took a step to see what was going on.

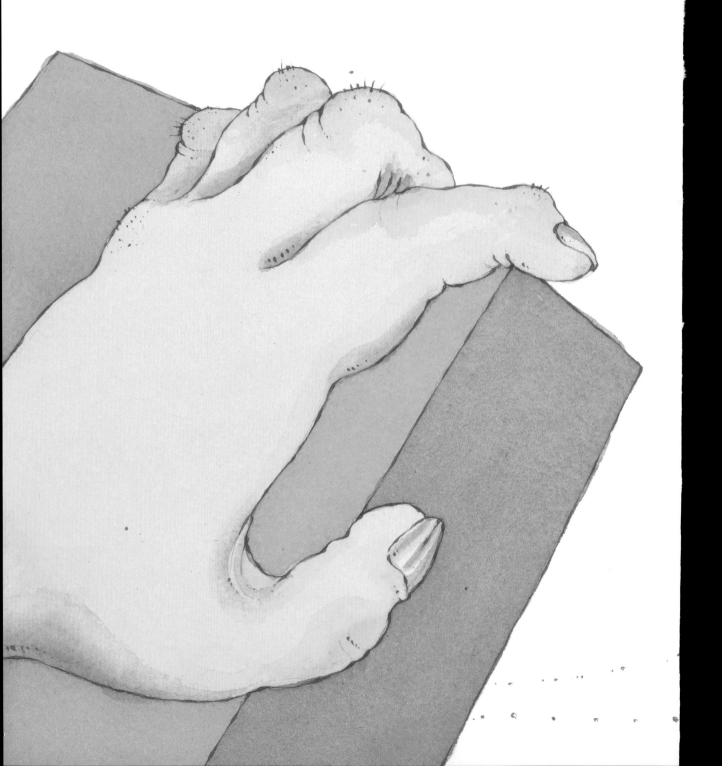

"NOW!" yelled the ant. Quickly, the moth turned and picked up the flea, while the fly picked up the ant, and they all started flying as fast as they could.

Big Jim saw what was happening and tried to grab them. He missed! So he began to close the circus box.

The moth and the fly and the flea and the ant kept flying, faster and faster. But not fast enough. Uh-oh!

As the circus lid came down, the ant, the fly, and the flea fell to the ground, with the fly's wing twisted and bent. Yes, they were outside the box, but what could they do now?

"Run!" cried the ant. "RUN!"

"Where's the moth?" asked the fly as they ran.

"He must be captured!" said the ant as Big Jim was about to scoop up the rest of them.

"We can't run fast enough," said the flea. "He's going to get us!"

But out of the blue, the moth came swooping down, and the ant, with all his might, threw the fly and the flea onto the moth's back. The three of them zoomed away.

"Wait, what about the ant?" asked the fly. "Shouldn't we do something?"

"THE ANT? That mean so-and-so, maybe he's finally getting what he—" the flea started to say, but then he stopped. No matter how mean he was, the flea thought, the ant was still his friend, and the fly's friend, and now, even the moth's friend.

And before he could say, "Let's turn back," the moth turned around and in the nick of time grabbed the ant and flew toward the full moon, *toward* the light.

"You know," said the ant, in the evening glow, "I could have been killed. I could have been stomped on. You, you almost left me! But . . . but . . . you didn't."

The ant, the fly, the flea, and the moth didn't say another word that night as they flew safely and quietly away.

They were friends, after all.